This book belongs to:

Liam and Fynn McNally
Thanksgiving 2015
With love and prayers,
Gramma and Poppa

PARABLE TREASURY

Liz Curtis Higgs

Illustrated by Nancy Munger

Tommy NELSON®

A Division of Thomas Nelson Publishers

NASHVILLE   MEXICO CITY   RIO DE JANEIRO

Parable Treasury
Text © 2015 by Liz Curtis Higgs
Illustrations © 2015 by Nancy Munger

Published in Nashville, Tennessee, by Tommy Nelson. Tommy Nelson is an imprint of Thomas Nelson. Thomas Nelson is a registered trademark of HarperCollins Christian Publishing, Inc.
Tommy Nelson titles may be purchased in bulk for educational, business, fund-raising, or sales promotional use. For information, please e-mail SpecialMarkets@ThomasNelson.com.

Scripture quotations are taken from the International Children's Bible®. Copyright © 1986, 1988, 1999 by Thomas Nelson. Used by permission. All rights reserved.

ISBN-13: 978-0-529-12067-0

Library of Congress Cataloging-in-Publication Data available for earlier editions under LC numbers 96-44222, 97-9998, 95-8000, 97-15570

Printed in China

15 16 17 18 19 DSC 6 5 4 3 2 1

Mfr: DSC / Shenzhen, China / September 2015 / PO # 9351527

ALL NEW MATERIAL
Filling: POLYURETHANE FOAM
REG. NO. PA-14954 (CA), MA-3031 (CN) MADE IN CHINA
TSSA Reg. No 07T-00912512

If you like

stories that make you smile,

pictures you can point to,

and words that fill you with wonder,

then this *Parable Treasury*

was written just for you!

CONTENTS

LETTER TO PARENTS

Dear Reader,

When God planted these stories in my heart, I never dreamed how many children and grandchildren, parents and grandparents, teachers and librarians, booksellers and book lovers would read them, season after season—all because you kindly shared these parables with your family and friends. Thanks so much!

You can be sure I chose each word with care and picked each Bible verse with prayer, hoping these simple stories would speak to young hearts of all ages.

The Pumpkin Patch Parable came first, a story that grew from my joy-filled experience of being made new in Christ. The other stories quickly followed, shared first with my own children, and then with you!

With all four parables in one volume, you'll have a new story ready to share each season. May God richly bless every minute you spend with a child by your side and a book in your hands.

Liz Curtis Higgs

The Parable
of the Lily

For Lillian Margaret Higgs,
our own Easter lily

One wintry day the farmer's young daughter shuffled through the snow, headed for the mailbox at the end of the lane.

B-r-r-r, it was cold!

She peered inside the mailbox and found a small white envelope. Surprise! It was addressed to her!

"Dear Maggie," the letter began. "I'm sending a very special gift just for you. Look for it soon!"

Maggie loved getting presents, especially a gift as mysterious as this one. When would it come? Who was it from? What would it be?

The farmer's daughter waited and waited . . . some days patiently, some days not so patiently.

Then one very ordinary afternoon, a box appeared on her doorstep. The gift had arrived!

So you also must be ready. The Son of Man will come at a time you don't expect him. Matthew 24:44

The farmer watched as his daughter excitedly tore off the wrapping paper. He was eager to see what she thought of her present.

But Maggie didn't say a word. She just stared at the small wooden crate full of dirt. Dirt was not at all what Maggie had hoped for!

Poking out of the soil was a small piece of paper that told Maggie how to care for her gift.

Hide in a cool, dark place.

Water as needed.

When spring comes, bring into the light.

Then she knew it must be a growing thing, like a bulb that would someday bloom into a plant.

He grew up like a small plant before the Lord.
He was like a root growing in a dry land. Isaiah 53:2

Oh dear. Her long-awaited gift wasn't
a toy or a doll or a game after all.

The farmer could see that his daughter
was very disappointed. His heart grew sad.
The gift was from him.

With a sigh, Maggie carried the wooden box down the steps into the darkest corner of the cellar and left it there on a shelf.

Sometimes she remembered to water it, but most of the time, Maggie just plain forgot.

He had no special beauty or form to make us notice him.   Isaiah 53:2

The farmer
did not forget.
He just waited.
And he watched.

Spring came at last.

The air was warmer, and the gray skies had melted into robin's egg blue. What a welcome sight the sun was!

It was time for the farmer to hoe his garden, getting the soil ready for the seeds that filled his pockets.

*In the same way the Lord God
will make grow what is right. Isaiah 61:11*

Maggie wanted to help, so she marched down the cellar steps to get her own Maggie-size gardening tools.

That's when it happened.

Searching for her toolbox in the darkest corner of the cellar, Maggie knocked the forgotten crate of dirt off the shelf.

Crash! The crate splintered into pieces, soil was everywhere, and the flower bulb that rolled to her feet showed no signs of life.

I tell you the truth. A [seed] must fall to the ground and die. Then it makes many seeds. John 12:24

What a mess! Maggie was mad at the box and even madder at herself. She swept up the dirt and threw away the broken box, grumbling under her breath.

He was hated and rejected by people. . . .
People would not even look at him. Isaiah 53:3

And that ugly old flower bulb?
She tossed it out the cellar
door, never to think of it again.

Until . . .

Maggie woke up earlier than usual Easter morning. A warm breeze blew through her bedroom window, and the chirping birds seemed to call her name.

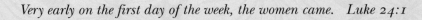

Very early on the first day of the week, the women came. Luke 24:1

Still dressed in her nightgown, Maggie tiptoed out into the garden. She was hoping to find some daffodils or tulips to decorate the table for Easter breakfast.

That's when she saw it. The loveliest lily that God ever made was blooming on the edge of her father's flower garden.

Thanks be to God for his gift that is too wonderful to explain.   2 Corinthians 9:15

Its white petals unfolded like a trumpet.
Its leaves were green with new life.
Its scent was as fragrant as the
most expensive perfume.

*But I tell you that even Solomon with his riches was not dressed
as beautifully as one of these flowers.* Matthew 6:29

Maggie knew all at once what had happened. She didn't know whether to laugh or cry or shout with joy. So Maggie did all three at once.

"Wake up, everybody! Wake up! Come see! The gift is alive!"

Her family hurried out to the garden. They couldn't believe their eyes! So much beauty from such an ugly box of dirt.

Maggie noticed the farmer standing in the doorway, quietly watching. His smile gave away his secret.

"Father, it was you who gave me the lily!" Maggie squealed with delight.

Suddenly her little girl smile began to fade. Oh dear.

She'd thrown away her father's gift without so much as a "thank you." How that must have hurt him!

But he took our suffering on him and felt our pain for us.   Isaiah 53:4

"I'm sorry, Daddy," she said, putting her little arms around his big waist. "Will you forgive me?"

"Oh, my child," the farmer whispered, hugging her tight. "That's what Easter is all about."

This is how God showed his love to us:
He sent his only Son into the world to give us life through him. 1 John 4:9

The Sunflower
Parable

For our tall, sunny son,
Matthew Logan Higgs

Logan whistled his way down the lane toward home. He was counting the days until the summer sun would shine on his very own corner of the garden.

The farmer promised him that he could plant
anything he wanted. And Logan wanted
something B-I-G, bigger than his brother's
cornstalks or his sister's hollyhocks. . . .

He wanted to grow great big sunflowers, so tall they would reach all the way to heaven!

After the warm sun of May chased the last frost away, Logan and the farmer chose the very best sunflower seeds.

God is the One who gives seed to the farmer. . . .
And God will give you all the seed you need and make it grow. 2 Corinthians 9:10

"GIANT" declared the seed packet. Logan was sure his sunflowers would touch the skies by August.

Seeds

GIANT

Logan and the farmer worked side by side. They hoed the hard soil. They cleared the heavy rocks. They yanked out the pesky weeds that might choke the plants.

A farmer does not plow his field all the time. . . .
He prepares the ground. Then he plants the . . . seed. Isaiah 28:24–25

The farmer added fertilizer. Logan pressed the tiny seeds down into the rich soil. Then the waiting began.

A farmer is patient. He waits for his valuable crop to grow from the earth. James 5:7

The warm summer rain brought fresh water. The sunflower seedlings poked their thirsty heads out of the soil.

"Drink! Drink!" Logan called from his window.

The hot summer sun brought warmth and light, which made the plants stretch taller.

"Grow! Grow!" Logan sang out.

How long until the flowers would bloom? How long until they reached heaven?

Soon everything in the garden was growing very tall indeed.

His brother's cornstalks soared up, up, up.

The deep springs of water made [them] tall.
Ezekiel 31:4

His sister's hollyhocks waved high above the fence.

But nothing grew taller than Logan's sunflowers.

Your love is so great it reaches to the skies.
Your truth reaches to the clouds. Psalm 57:10

Whenever a breeze blew through the garden, the sunflowers nodded their heads.

"Yes!" they seemed to say. "We have B-I-G plans this summer."

July turned into August without making a sound. The giant flowers turned their blossoms toward heaven. They followed the sun with their own round, brown faces.

"Soon my sunflowers will stretch all the way to heaven," Logan boasted. He was very proud of his hard work.

You know that your work in the Lord is never wasted.
1 Corinthians 15:58

But at summer's end, the flowers suddenly stopped growing. Their faces, heavy with seeds, bent toward the ground.

Hungry birds hopped around the stalks.

Logan grew very sad. The tallest flowers on his father's farm would never make it to heaven now.

The tall corn would be cut down for harvest.

The hollyhocks would soon bloom no more.

All their work was good for nothing.

What do people really gain from
all the hard work they do here on earth? Ecclesiastes 1:3

The farmer knew his son was disappointed, but the farmer also knew a secret or two:

The corn would provide food for many people.

The hollyhocks would bloom again next summer.

And the sunflowers . . . ?

Well, the sunflowers were created with a gift inside: SEEDS! Seeds to feed birds. Seeds to feed people. Seeds to be carried all over the world, just as God planned.

The plants make seeds for the farmer. And from these seeds people have [food] to eat.
The words I say do the same thing. They will not return to me empty.
They make the things happen that I want to happen. They succeed in doing what I send them to do. Isaiah 55:10–11

"Look, my son," the farmer said. "See what a good harvest your sunflowers have produced."

Logan watched as birds of every kind lifted the seeds right out of the sunflowers. The birds flew up, up, over the fields, off toward the horizon until they disappeared from sight.

"Father, the sunflowers reached heaven after all!" Logan shouted with joy. "Those seeds will go everywhere."

Everywhere in the world that Good News
is bringing blessings and is growing. Colossians 1:6

The farmer nodded. "What can you do with the sunflower seeds that are left?"

Finish the work that you started.
Then your "doing" will be equal to your "wanting to do." 2 Corinthians 8:11

Logan thought harder. "We can sprinkle our seeds with salt and share them with hungry friends!"

Because we loved you, we were happy to share God's Good News with you. 1 Thessalonians 2:8

"And we can save some seeds to plant next summer," Logan said, pleased with himself for thinking such good thoughts. "Next year, let's plant twice as many seeds!"

Remember this: The person who plants a little will have a small harvest.
But the person who plants a lot will have a big harvest. 2 Corinthians 9:6

The farmer nodded once more and smiled. "See how much good we can do when we work together in my garden?"

The Pumpkin Patch Parable

A Note to Parents from the Author

This story is NOT a celebration of Halloween . . . no ghosts, goblins, demons, witches, or monsters here!

As a mother, I wanted to offer an alternative message for our kids each autumn, something wholesome, positive and encouraging. Since the Lord himself created pumpkins, it seemed appropriate to redeem this familiar symbol of the harvest season for his good purpose.

My prayer is that through this simple pumpkin parable your own heart will be filled with the light of God's love and you, too, will let yourself glow!

See that big red barn? And those rolling green fields? That's where the farmer lives, w-a-a-a-y out in the country. It's so far out the streets don't even have stop signs.

Fresh Vegetables

The farmer grows many different things in his fields.
He grows tall green corn and big red tomatoes . . .

long yellow squash and little green peas.
People eat that stuff for dinner.

I am the true vine; my Father is the gardener. John 15:1

The BEST vegetables the farmer grows are PUMPKINS! They start out as flat, oval seeds, almost as big as raisins.

The kingdom of heaven is like a man who planted good seed in his field. Matthew 13:24

One hot June day soon after school was out, the farmer planted his pumpkin seeds, just like he did every summer.

The seeds disappeared into the ground in neat rows and grew there in the dark, all through the Fourth of July.

Early one morning, a tiny green shoot quietly poked its way out of the soil. Soon, a long, green vine stretched across the ground. From that vine, little buds sprouted into wide green leaves.

The leaves spread out flat to catch the August sun.

Someday, those little green buds would turn into big orange pumpkins!

But not yet. The patient farmer waited. And waited.

God is being patient with you. He does not want anyone to be lost. He wants everyone to change his heart and life. 2 Peter 3:9

The pumpkins began to grow. How different they looked!

Some were tall and lean.

Some were short and round.

Some had lumps and bumps.

ALL of them were pumpkins!

October came at last. Every night grew dark earlier than the night before, and the farmer knew it was harvesttime. His workers brought in the ripe pumpkins. Which one would the farmer choose?

Open your eyes. Look at the fields that are ready for harvesting now. John 4:35

75

The farmer picked up one large pumpkin, taking great care. Pumpkins are tough on the outside but break into smithereens if dropped. He washed off all the dirt, holding on tight.

Next came the messy part. The pumpkin was filled with seeds and slimy pulp. The farmer had a special plan for his chosen pumpkin, so the seeds and slime would have to go.

Create in me a pure heart, God. Psalm 51:10

He slowly cut all the way around the top of the pumpkin. Gently, he pulled the stem.

God's word is alive and working. It is sharper than a sword sharpened on both sides.
It cuts all the way into us. . . . And God's word judges the thoughts
and feelings in our hearts. Hebrews 4:12

Now the farmer could look inside. Squishy, stringy pulp waited for him . . . yuck!

The farmer pulled out all the slimy pulp and wrapped it up in an old newspaper. Off to the compost pile it went, never to be seen again.

Then, something
REALLY
exciting happened:
the pumpkin got a new face!

The farmer carved a triangle for each eye. Pumpkins have eyes that don't blink or turn away. They see everything!

The eye is a light for the body. If your eyes are good, then your whole body will be full of light. Matthew 6:22

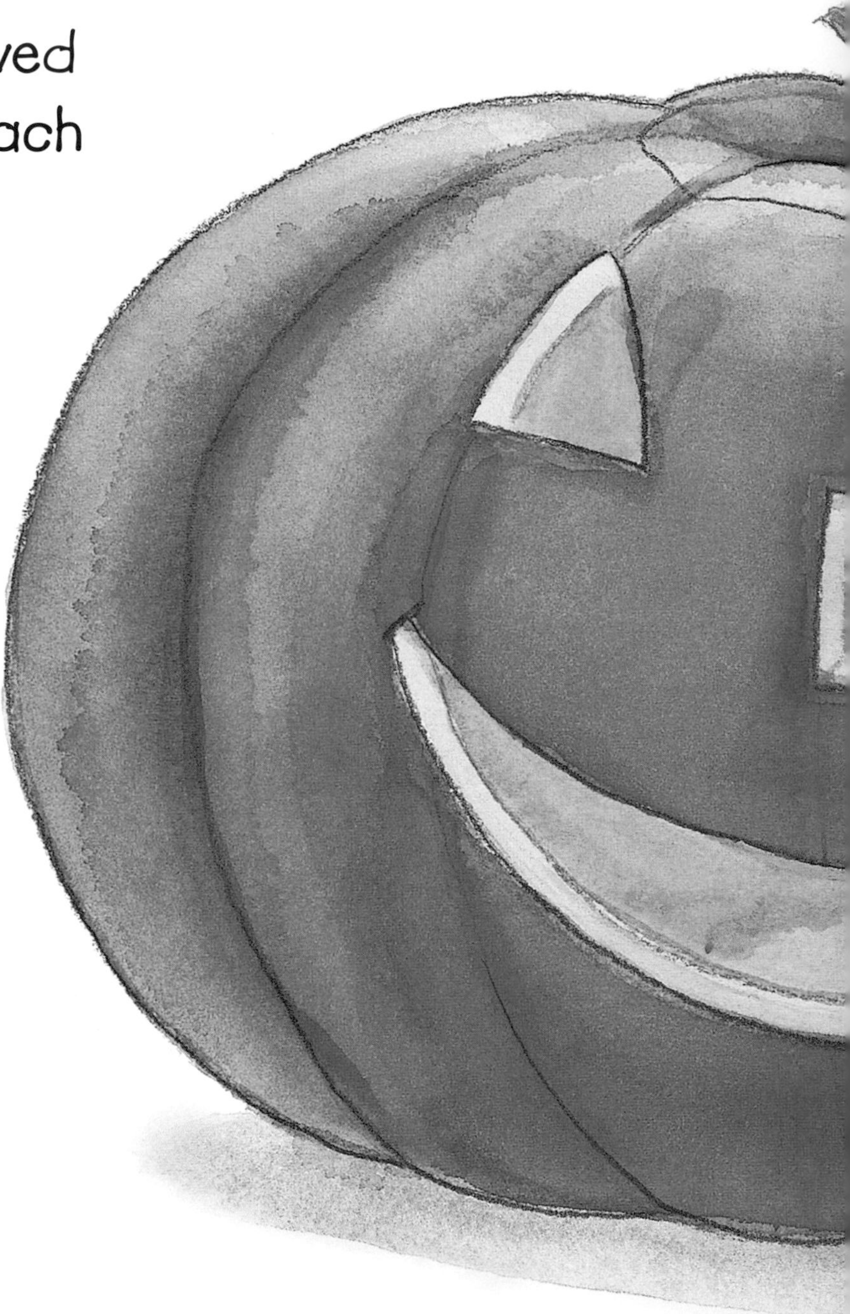

He neatly made
a little square
for the nose,
and then
he carved
a big,
w-i-d-e
smile.

Happiness makes a person smile. Proverbs 15:13

83

The farmer put a small candle inside his pumpkin and touched the wick with a flame. How that pumpkin glowed!

God once said, "Let the light shine out of the darkness!" And this is the same God who made his light shine in our hearts. 2 Corinthians 4:6

The pumpkin on the porch shone brightly for everyone to see. When people saw the smiling pumpkin, they all smiled back!

In the same way, you should be a light for other people.
Live so that they will see the good things you do. Live so that
they will praise your Father in heaven. Matthew 5:16

All the neighbors knew that, once again, the farmer had turned a simple pumpkin into a simply glorious sight.

In the same way. God the Father offers His children the chance to be made new, full of joy and full of light, shining like stars in a dark world.

The Pine Tree
Parable

For Matthew and Lillian
-Liz Curtis Higgs

For Jessica and Joshua
-Nancy Munger Anderson

Every spring, the farmer planted flowers. Every summer, he grew fruits and vegetables. Every fall, he harvested bright orange pumpkins.

Fresh Produce

And every day of every year, the farmer grew the tallest, widest, biggest, greenest, loveliest crop of all . . .

. . . Christmas trees!

He plants a pine tree, and the rain makes it grow.
Isaiah 44:14

The farmer and his wife began planting seedlings when their children were small. Each year the family grew. So did the little pine trees.

The trees were quiet. The children were noisy.
But the farmer's wife loved everything that
grew on the farm.

One chilly November day, the time finally came to sell the pine trees to the neighbors.

People bought the fine looking trees, which soon filled many homes with the fragrance of Christmas.

Let each of us please his neighbor for his good, to help him be stronger in faith. Romans 15:2

But the farmer's wife couldn't bear to part with one remarkable tree. It stood very tall and perfectly straight. Its long branches danced on the wintry air.

The farmer's wife hung a tag on the pine tree: NOT FOR SALE. She added a shiny gold star on top. Now the family could enjoy the tree day after day, year after year, Christmas after Christmas.

So the tree was great and beautiful, with its long branches. Its roots reached down to many waters.   Ezekiel 31:7

The next holiday season brought more neighbors to the farm. The perfect tree was taller than ever.

NOT FOR SALE

So the tree was taller than all the other trees of the field.   Ezekiel 31:5

Trees & Wreaths

When the neighbors asked, "Ooh, how much for this beautiful tree?" the farmer's wife just smiled and shook her head.

"Sorry. Not for sale."

It cannot even be bought with the purest gold.   Job 28:19

One Christmas Eve when the farmer's children were children no longer, a family of three drove up in a rusty old truck.

Their clothes were patched, and their faces looked tired.

You will always have the poor with you. Matthew 26:11

103

They trudged up and down a row of trees that no one else wanted. The trees had missing branches and crooked trunks.

Those trees were
free. They were the only kind of Christmas
tree the family could afford.

The little child found her way to the tallest pine tree. She stood at the foot of it, looking up, up through the sweeping branches to the glistening star on top.

"Oh, my!" she sang out. "Can we buy this one?"

Her parents were embarrassed. They knew they could never afford it. The farmer's family was also embarrassed. They knew too.

But the little girl didn't know the cost. She only knew it was the most wonderful pine tree in the world. "Please?" was all she could say.

It is sad when you don't get what you hoped for. Proverbs 13:12

The little girl was so poor yet so full of hope. What could the farmer's wife say to her? What could she do?

The farmer's wife took a deep breath. "I'm sorry," she said. "This tree is not for sale. But we'd like you to have it . . . as a gift."

Being kind to the poor is like lending to the Lord.
The Lord will reward you for what you have done. Proverbs 19:17

The little girl's parents could not speak a word. What a kind and generous gift! The farmer's wife did not even know them. They were strangers.

The whole law is made complete in this one command: "Love your neighbor as you love yourself." Galatians 5:14

The farmer smiled at his wife. "Well done," his smile seemed to say. "The gift is good."

As the farmer took his saw to the bottom of
the trunk, the child could not keep her joy inside.

She leaped up and down. "Hooray! Hooray! The
tree is ours!"

*When wishes come true, it's like
eating fruit from the tree of life. Proverbs 13:12*

The farmer's wife watched her favorite pine tree as it fell to the snowy ground. Tears shone in her eyes. She brushed them away like snowflakes.

Yes, it was a great sacrifice. But it brought even greater joy.

Isn't that just like Christmas?